How Little Coyote Found His Secret Strength

Anne Westcott and C. C. Alicia Hu

Illustrated by Ching-Pang Kuo

Jessica Kingsley Publishers
London and Philadelphia

First published in 2018
by Jessica Kingsley Publishers
73 Collier Street
London N1 9BE, UK
and
400 Market Street, Suite 400
Philadelphia, PA 19106, USA

www.jkp.com

Copyright © Anne Westcott and C. C. Alicia Hu 2018
Introduction copyright © Pat Ogden 2018

Library of Congress Cataloging in Publication Data
A CIP catalog record for this book is available from the
Library of Congress

British Library Cataloguing in Publication Data
A CIP catalogue record for this book is available from
the British Library

ISBN 978 1 78592 770 6
eISBN 978 1 78450 670 4

Printed and bound in China

books in the same series

Bomji and Spotty's Frightening Adventure
A Story About How to Recover
From a Scary Experience
ISBN 978 1 78592 770 6
eISBN 978 1 78450 670 4

How Sprinkle the Pig Escaped the River of Tears
A Story About Being Apart From Loved Ones
ISBN 978 1 78592 769 0
eISBN 978 1 78450 669 8

Introduction

The body possesses innate capacities to ensure we make it through distressing situations. This inborn wisdom of the body inspired me to develop Sensorimotor Psychotherapy℠ (SP) decades ago. I have made it my life's work to elucidate this largely untapped resource so that we can engage it to help ourselves and others heal from severe stress, trauma, and attachment disruption.

The Hidden Strengths Therapeutic Children's Books series captures this essential spirit and intention of Sensorimotor Psychotherapy℠. The authors render the core concepts of this approach accessible to both caregivers and young people struggling in the aftermath of overwhelming experiences. The stories do so with sensitivity and particular attention to illustrating the bodily experience of the child in an engaging and compelling manner.

Understanding the language of the body helps us make sense of the often confusing behaviors following trauma and separation from loved ones. We freeze, run away, collapse, fight, hide, cry for someone bigger and wiser to help us, and even dissociate or do things we wouldn't normally do, like steal, to make it through. These instinctive bodily survival defenses are automatically engaged in times of threat. Each of us employs the defensive response(s) that will work best in a particular moment given the immediate circumstances, so there is no single best survival strategy. These compelling stories emphasize the hidden strengths in the characters' survival behaviors, staying true to the foundational principle of SP that the physical actions taken are the person's best attempt to respond to the situation they face.

Over time, we develop habits of defensive responses, often repeatedly engaging just one or two survival defenses. These then become our default behaviors in the face of subsequent threats, which is compassionately and wisely illustrated by the appealing characters in the stories in the series. Anyone helping children will find new ways to look at the often challenging and misunderstood behaviors children display after stress. The stories also encourage caregivers and children to become curious about the survival functions these behaviors may serve.

As the authors, both trained in Sensorimotor Psychotherapy℠, describe how the characters adapt to challenging circumstances, the body's wisdom is revealed. Each character favors a different survival defense, which is cleverly portrayed through the character's movement, posture, and physiology. The pictures and rich descriptive text convey the real-life bodily and emotional experience of so many children, without evaluation, judgement, or interpretation. The stories describe events and behaviors from each character's viewpoint, offering a variety of perspectives. Doing so enhances understanding of how the body responds and influences the meaning we make of what we see, hear, and feel. The ability to gain perspective, to stay curious, and to experiment are core to Sensorimotor Psychotherapy℠ and woven into each story. Children will feel relieved and understood as they recognize themselves and their peers in the myriad struggles of the characters. Behaviors children might have perceived as ineffective or worse, a confirmation of their own badness, may very well be transformed into a strength that can be adapted to help them thrive. Our bodies adapt via movement, posture, and physiology.

The supplements following the stories will help caregivers recognize the signs of these survival strengths in the simple body clues of gesture, posture, tone of voice, facial expression, eye gaze, and movement. This is what I have termed the "somatic narrative" core to Sensorimotor Psychotherapy℠. When one understands the language the body uses to tell the story of distress, puzzling and confusing behaviors by children begin to make more sense. When we can make sense of our children's behaviors, we are better equipped to respond in flexible and sensitive ways to help our children feel better in their bodies, hearts, and minds.

Pat Ogden, Founder, Sensorimotor Psychotherapy Institute, 2017

About the Hidden Strengths Series

This book is part of a series for children who have lived through extremely stressful times. The series is inspired by Sensorimotor Psychotherapy℠, a unique approach to trauma treatment developed by Dr. Pat Ogden. The series is designed to present children's distress in a realistic yet digestible way.

The authors have carefully crafted the stories so as to reduce sensory stimulus and not overwhelm traumatized children. You will notice this in the language chosen: simple yet descriptive, in a way that seeks to highlight hidden strengths in potentially shaming moments. You will also see this in the images as they shift away from bright color to grays at particularly tense moments. The very crafting of the book was guided by the principles and knowledge of Sensorimotor Psychotherapy℠ and the authors' deep understanding of children. This attention to the reader's experience makes the book useful to anyone caring for traumatized children.

We possess many kinds of strengths to get through challenging times. Some are obvious and some are harder to see. Many of these hidden strengths live in our bodies and leap to our rescue instantly, bypassing our thinking. These strengths try to keep us safe in times of danger when we have to act fast and may not have help around.

These books will help you and your child gain understanding and appreciation for the amazing abilities that live inside of you. By sharing these stories with your child, these books will help them to reduce feelings of shame, recognize that problematic feelings and behaviors can be a response to stressful times, and feel better in their body.

OTHER BOOKS IN THE SERIES

You and your child will meet several characters over and over again when you explore the series. The animals' lives intertwine in unexpected ways. Gaining a deeper window into each character changes our feelings toward the animals. The series is crafted to generate curiosity, empathy, and perspective-taking in the reader. These capacities are stunted by trauma and chronic stress.

READING TIPS

Find a space where you are both in a relaxed and playful mood. Allow 20–30 minutes to explore and talk about the content.

1. Allow children to decide the reading speed. Some children enjoy exploring the details in pictures more than the storyline. Some children may have emotional reactions to the content and want to skip or fast-forward to a later part of the story.

2. Children are very creative. Your child may ask questions you can't answer. Support your child's curiosity by encouraging them to come up with their own answers.

3. Suggested activities are provided at the end of each book. They are designed to help deepen the learning from the story through all your child's senses.

In the deep dark forest, there lived a gang of coyotes. The coyotes were all big and tough... Well, all except one—Little Coyote.

The bigger coyotes were mean to Little Coyote. For as long as Little Coyote could remember, everyone had called him Wimpy.

His real name was long forgotten.

Biggest Coyote barked, "Wimpy, come pick up the trash!"

Little Coyote had learned to keep safe by following orders.
It was better not to attract any attention. If he did, the others
only bullied him even more.

"Wimpy, go get two eggs for me!"

Little Coyote didn't really want to do this, so he would take the long, slow trail to the chicken coop.

On his walk, he would explore the quiet corners of the forest.

"Wimpy, come here! I want to practice my boxing."

Little Coyote had learned how to let his muscles go soft and his mind go far away when the others wanted to box.

This hidden ability to go away helped Little Coyote get through hard times.

All day long, the big coyotes barked orders at Little Coyote.

Little Coyote mumbled, "Oh... Okay..."

A hidden strength lived in his body: he instantly became small, his shoulders hunched, and his voice disappeared whenever he was near the big coyotes.

This hidden strength helped Little Coyote to stay near to the mean bigger coyotes without them noticing and bullying him. He was too young to live on his own.

After a while Little Coyote decided he wanted to get away from the other coyotes and explore.

He learned that using his hidden strength, he could slip away unnoticed by the bigger coyotes. This way, he could enjoy some peace and quiet in the forest for a little while.

One day, when at the edge of the forest, he heard the faint twinkle of playful voices. Curious, he followed the sounds.

Little Coyote was excited and a bit nervous. "Who is this in my forest?" he wondered.

Little Coyote spotted a little boy rabbit and a little girl cat happily picking flowers together. Little Coyote was puzzled by their kind voices.

"Maybe, oh maybe, they might be friends with me," hoped Little Coyote.

As Little Coyote walked toward them, the rabbit and cat froze, and their voices stopped.

Then, suddenly, the cat jumped out and yelled, "Hey, I'll bet you can't run as fast as I can!"

The cat quickly ran off down the path.

As always, Little Coyote did what he was ordered.

He dashed after the cat.

Soon, the cat scrambled up a nearby tree. She climbed higher and higher!

Little Coyote tried to climb after her, but coyotes cannot climb.

Embarrassment swallowed Little Coyote. He knew he had failed again.

His heart sank as he slunk away into the forest.

A little voice inside him said, "What if the other coyotes saw me? They will laugh at me, again."

Little Coyote scurried back to his cave.

Once there, he thought, "I'm so useless! The other coyotes are right to call me Wimpy!"

His body crumpled and he longed to disappear, so no one could ever laugh at him again.

The next day, Little Coyote's tummy turned upside down and he held his breath when he saw the other coyotes. "Uh oh, do they know? Did they see I could not catch a cat?"

Then, a big coyote barked, "Go get me a chicken egg!"

Little Coyote took a deep breath of relief. The big coyotes were treating him the same as always.

"Phew, they must not have seen that I messed up," he thought. Things were back to usual!

As Little Coyote crept toward the chicken coop, his body instantly used its ability to move sneakily. Mama Chicken did not see or hear him approach.

Quick as a flash, Little Coyote snatched the fattest egg in the nest. "Wow, I am getting better and better at gathering eggs," he thought. That made Little Coyote feel warm inside and grow taller.

As Little Coyote heard Mama Chicken's upset squawks his heart felt a sharp twinge, but he couldn't stop—he had to get back to the big coyotes.

Tired from his busy day, Little Coyote went home to his cozy cave. There he fell into a deep sleep.

In his dream, Little Coyote was running free!

Moon gazed through the window at Little Coyote dreaming, as she had every night since Little Coyote was born.

In his dream, Little Coyote raced and his friends cheered. Suddenly his body felt strong and powerful; his legs pumped like pistons. This was so unfamiliar.

His legs ran faster and faster. The wind rushed through his fur as he zoomed through the forest.

He had not forgotten how to be strong even after all that time being small and following orders.

He was grinning from ear to ear; he didn't think about winning or losing—he just thought about how great he felt.

He was running side by side with his new friend, Cat. Together they crossed the finish line, tired out and happy.

As Little Coyote dreamed on, Moon sighed. She knew that when he woke up in the morning he would face the big coyotes again.

Moon saw Little Coyote's true nature. She understood that while living with the bigger coyotes, Little Coyote had to keep his inner strengths deeply hidden.

She trusted Little Coyote would one day grow up to be a true hero and leave the bigger coyotes. Maybe then it would be safe for him to walk strong and tall.

Moon breathed loving kindness upon Little Coyote, as she had done every night since he was born. Tonight, she sent him a song to remind him of his body's strength.

Little Coyote, run, run, run. Your friends, they cheer!

How warm you feel! How happy you are!

Your friends see your true nature.

Before the time is right, keep close your secret strength.

Safe inside, hidden it thrives.

Little Coyote, run, run, run. Your body running free!

How tall you feel! How strong you are!

The world needs your bravery now.

When the time is right, take a stand, speak the truth.

May you claim back your true name...

Let's Talk About Little Coyote's Secret Strengths

Remember how Little Coyote's body would become small and his voice would go quiet around the big coyotes? Sometimes we have to be with people we don't like or feel comfortable with. At these times our bodies know how to get small and follow orders. This is sometimes called "submitting." We all have this skill built into our bodies.

How was getting small helpful to Little Coyote? When would it be smart to keep quiet when someone speaks to you?

How could Little Coyote feel good about stealing Mama Chicken's eggs?

To live among the big coyotes, he had practiced and become very good at moving quietly so as not to be noticed. This made him very good at gathering food. He was proud of his skill.

Little Coyote only felt a small twinge of guilt about stealing. He was so used to having his feelings ignored by the other coyotes that he hadn't learnt how to understand others' feelings, including Mama Chicken's.

Moving very quietly is a strength for Little Coyote, but when could this strength become a problem for him?

Play Time

MAKE UP YOUR OWN ENDING FOR LITTLE COYOTE

Now, you get to be the storyteller. You get to decide what happens next! You could:

Put on a play.
Write your own ending.
Tell your story to an adult and have them write it down.
Draw your ending.

IDEAS

You can use the following ideas to inspire you as you create a new ending for Little Coyote.

Magic Power

What magic powers would you want Moon to give Little Coyote?

How would these powers help Little Coyote when he wakes up?

Hidden Strengths

What hidden strength would you choose if you were Little Coyote?

How would this hidden strength help you to live with the bigger coyotes?

Friendship Matters

Little Coyote dreamed of having new friends and running free in the woods. Invent a story of how you would make new friends if you were Little Coyote. How would you want your friends to help you if you were having a hard time?

Loving Kindness

Can you sing a song to share with Little Coyote that would help make him feel a little better?

Is there a new soothing song your adult would like to teach you?

Guide for Grown-Ups

NEW VOCABULARY AND STORY GUIDE

This story is about a brave young coyote who lives with a gang of tough older coyotes. He struggles to find his way, learning to steal and yield to the demands of others in order to survive. Adults can misunderstand these behaviors, failing to see their usefulness at one point in children's lives. Please help children to see that all of what Little Coyote did were hidden strengths. In some environments, all of us may resort to similar actions to survive.

HIDDEN STRENGTH: SUBMISSION

This strength allows Little Coyote to stay near his gang of coyotes.

page 9

Little Coyote lives in a rough world. He has to cope with bigger coyotes' cruel behaviors. Because Little Coyote is the smallest and weakest, he cannot fight or run away. If Little Coyote fights he will lose; if Little Coyote runs away, he won't survive on his own.

Sometimes, when we are very scared our bodies become frozen. In the animal world, opossums are famous for feigning death: when they appear dead, they are less desirable to a predator. Deer are famous for standing still in the woods, allowing themselves to blend into the scenery and become less visible to the roving eye of a predator.

But Little Coyote also needs to respond to the bigger coyotes' demands, so he cannot simply freeze or feign death. Instead, he uses a different smart defense: simply doing what he is told. Little Coyote learns to cope by being *submissive*.

By "collapsing" his body, Little Coyote makes himself look small and non-threatening. By following the orders without thinking, Little Coyote avoids any conflict that could bring him danger. While they're different from "strengths" as we might conventionally imagine them, these are Little Coyote's hidden strengths.

However, if we submit over and over again, it can become a habit we can't stop using, even when we may not need it. Just like Little Coyote, if we collapse our core body, we tend to give up easily and blame ourselves.

HIDDEN STRENGTH: STEALTH

Moving sneakily and quietly enables Little Coyote to get away from bigger coyotes or take eggs. Remember, without this ability Little Coyote would get a hard time from the bigger coyotes.

page 7

We all know we need to teach children not to steal, so it can be hard to accept how Little Coyote's strength enables him to steal and to feel proud doing so.

However, to help children recover from harsh environments, we must challenge ourselves to see the world through *their* eyes. To understand a child's perspective we need to imagine how we would move through the world in their body—in their size and shape—and to experience the feelings they have experienced.

Little Coyote experiences a sharp twinge when he steals the eggs, but his fear of the other coyotes and the pride he has in doing a job well leads him to ignore the feeling.

As adults, it's important that we avoid shaming a traumatized child for such behavior. Reducing a child's feelings of shame is the first step toward helping them to build healthy judgement and moral character. This step is often missed by adults. Adults can move to teaching right from wrong too quickly.

Traumatized children are easily overwhelmed by feelings of shame. When children begin to feel a twinge of shame, they often act out, rage, or tune out.

However, when we are able to identify and explain to a child how they used their hidden strengths to survive, children feel our understanding and compassion and don't feel judged or punished. This sense of security allows the child's feelings of remorse and guilt to surface. Children build a sense of security and safety from feeling badly without feeling shamed. This felt sense of trust paves the way for adults to help children learn new ways to get what they need.

HIDDEN STRENGTH: SELF-CONFIDENCE AND BODY STRENGTH

In the story, Little Coyote discovers another hidden strength—his inner confidence and power in his body. In Little Coyote's dream, he no longer has a collapsed body. He runs fearlessly. His spine lengthens, the front of his body opens up, and there is energy in his limbs.

A strong inner confidence comes when he feels his body's strength and the joy of moving. This inner confidence remains like a seed dormant inside while he survives his dangerous world. Moon shares a look into the future where Little Coyote will stand tall, feel his confidence, and rediscover his real name.

page 14

HIDDEN STRENGTH: ADULTS AND FRIENDS AS SECURE SUPPORT

In his dream, Little Coyote plays with different animal friends in the forest. His dream world is not like his tough reality. It's not about being the boss and winning. Little Coyote dreams of a peaceful forest where running is about playing and connecting with friends. This natural tendency to connect is one of Little Coyote's hidden strengths, keeping him hopeful and feeling loved.

In this story, Moon has looked down on Little Coyote as he sleeps since he was born. As caregiving adults, we are the steady attentive others who watch over our children and hold them in mind and heart.

Sometimes we adults know a child will go back to a difficult situation after spending time with us. However, just like Moon

page 21

singing to Little Coyote, we can help by sitting with children in their distress. We can help them pay attention to their own hidden strengths. We can help children reconnect with their body's strength by lengthening their spine to stand tall or doing a push-up to feel the power in their arms.

In addition, this caring relationship is an external resource. We need to find ways to help children remember this relationship when we are apart. A small stone, a picture, or an article of clothing might be appreciated by a child—something to remind them that they are cared for.

Anne Westcott's life work focuses on helping people (young and old) who have been having a hard time to understand how their bodies give them hidden strengths. She is a clinical social worker and psychotherapist who lives in Concord, Massachusetts with her husband and two daughters, and she loves to be outside and moving, no matter what the weather.

Growing up with manga (comics) in Taiwan, **C. C. Alicia Hu** knows the secret of learning new things is to look at words and pictures together. That's why she enjoys making stories like this series! As a practicing psychologist in Moscow, Idaho and Pullman, Washington, she also enjoys using simple body exercises to help people feel better about themselves.

BOMJI AND SPOTTY'S FRIGHTENING ADVENTURE

A Story About How to Recover from a Scary Experience

One sunny day, Bomji the Rabbit and his friend Spotty the Cat meet something very scary while picking flowers in the woods.

The friends manage to escape, but afterward Bomji just doesn't feel safe anymore. His body feels a bit different and he starts to have bad dreams. His friend Spotty is worried about Bomji – how can her friend be helped? Luckily, wise Teacher Owl is there for them.

This therapeutic picture book allows children and adults to talk about a frightening experience. The story is followed by helpful guidance for adults on how to help your child. It explores how your body and how you feel are affected by scary experiences, and explains how you can use your body to help to recover too.

HOW SPRINKLE THE PIG ESCAPED THE RIVER OF TEARS

A Story About Being Apart from Loved Ones

Sprinkle the Pig has moved to a new house with a new family, but he misses his old family. On his first day at school his classmate yells at him, and everything gets too much. He cries and cries, and soon the tears become a river and carry him away! Wise monkey spots Sprinkle, but he is too far away. Can he help Sprinkle to find hidden strengths to survive the river of tears?

This therapeutic picture book is written to help children aged 4–10 and adults to talk about being separated from or losing loved ones, and explores how difficult experiences can affect how your body feels and reacts to things. It is followed by easy to read advice for adults on how to help your child.

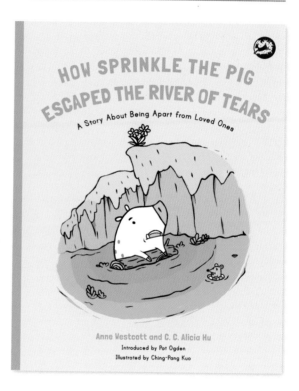

HOW SPRINKLE THE PIG ESCAPED THE RIVER OF TEARS

A Story About Being Apart from Loved Ones

Anne Westcott and C. C. Alicia Hu

Introduced by Pat Ogden

Illustrated by Ching-Pang Kuo